VEXOS INVASION

BY TRACEY WEST

SCHOLASTIC INC.

NEW YORK   TORONTO   LONDON   AUCKLAND
SYDNEY   MEXICO CITY   NEW DELHI   HONG KONG

ISBN 978-0-545-17760-3

© SPIN MASTER LTD/SEGA TOYS.

12 11 10 9 8 7 6 5 4 3 2 1   10 11 12 13 14 15/0
                                                      40
INTERIOR DESIGNED BY HENRY NG
PRINTED IN THE U.S.A.
FIRST PRINTING, MAY 2010

A terrible accident divided the planet Vestroia into six different worlds. This alternate dimension was populated by Bakugan, creatures with amazing powers. When a portal opened up between Vestroia and Earth, humans created a game using the Bakugan and their powers.

That's how Dan Kuso met his Bakugan Drago. They battled together to save Earth from a power-seeking Bakugan. Then Drago united the six planets of Vestroia by sacrificing himself to become the core of New Vestroia.

Dan missed Drago, but knowing that the Bakugan had found peace on their home world made him happy.

Of course, all good things must come to an end. . . .

It was a beautiful morning on New Vestroia. Bakugan freely roamed the land, enjoying the sparkling sunshine and fresh air.

Ventus Falconeer, a birdlike Bakugan with large, green wings, soared across the blue sky. Subterra Juggernoid, a Bakugan with a shell like a turtle, swam peacefully in the clean, bubbling waters of a flowing river. Pyrus Saurus admired the giant flowers growing on the riverbank, deeply sniffing their scent. On a nearby rock, Aquos Sirenoid dangled her fish tail in the water and strummed a happy melody on her harp.

Suddenly, a warm wind kicked up and a shadow fell over the land. The Bakugan looked up to see seven ships descending from the sky.

The spinning ships were dome-shaped. Six smaller ships circled the largest one. They hovered in midair at first, and then metal legs emerged and the ships planted themselves on the ground.

A metal rod with a globe on top extended from the top of the largest ship. The globe began to spin, shooting waves of rainbow-colored energy in every direction.

"By the spirits!" Sirenoid cried out.

The energy rays swept the Bakugan into the air. They screamed in panic as the energy caused them to transform into Bakugan balls.

"They've trapped us!" Sirenoid yelled.

She and the other Bakugan struggled to free themselves, but it was no use. As the balls bounced back to the ground, small ships zipped through the sky, sending out beams of sparkling light. The light picked up the Bakugan and carried them into the ship.

"Noooooooooo!" the Bakugan cried.

Back on Earth, Dan was walking down a crowded city sidewalk. Video advertisements played on billboards, cars whizzed past on the street, and people rushed around, talking and laughing.

Then Dan noticed something. The city grew quiet, people stopped moving, and cars came to a halt.

"Everything's slowing down," Dan said, looking around. He had experienced this before, at the start of a Bakugan battle. Time and space would freeze around the battlefield.

Then the sunny sky went dark, and a huge, glowing planet appeared in the sky.

"Am I seeing things?" Dan asked out loud. "Is that . . . Vestroia?"

Colors swirled on the planet's surface — blue, green, yellow, red. Then the light exploded, and Dan shielded his eyes. When he looked up again, the blue sky was back, and the planet looked like a large, glowing orb. It slowly faded from view and time started up again, and the people and cars around him began to move.

"That was weird," Dan remarked. "Something's not right. I can feel it."

CHAPTER 2

TIGRERRA FALLS

W *eeks later . . .*

Two brawlers faced off under the skies of New Vestroia.

Spectra floated above the battlefield, a tall figure in a long, red coat with a black feathered collar. His blond hair was long and wavy, and he wore a red mask over his eyes.

His opponent, Baron, was a few years younger. His purple spiky hair stuck straight up out of his red headband.

Spectra's Bakugan Helios rose up behind his master, spreading his large wings. A dragonoid with Darkus powers, Helios had black scales all over his body, fierce claws, and a mouth full of sharp fangs.

"Give up, Baron?" Spectra asked. Helios roared loudly.

"As if!" Baron yelled boldly, as his Haos Nemus burst up from the ground. Nemus was a humanoid Bakugan with a gleaming body and gold, angelic wings. In his right hand, he held a long golden staff topped with a gold circle that had five golden spikes sticking out around it.

"Ability Activate!" Baron called out. "Pyra-might! Skid Roa!"

Beams of golden light poured from the spikes, forming a pyramid-shaped protective wall around Nemus.

Spectra grinned. "Take them, Helios," he said. "Ability Activate. Burst Core!"

Helios roared as two balls of fire formed in each of his front claws. He charged at the glowing pyramid and tore it apart with his burning hands. Then he launched a wave of flame at Nemus.

Nemus slammed onto the battlefield, defeated.

He was Spectra's Bakugan now.

"Nemus!" Baron wailed.

A white Bakugan ball floated in front of Baron's face. The ball opened up to reveal a Bakugan that looked like a white tiger.

It was Haos Tigrerra. Back on Earth, Tigrerra had battled with Dan's friend Runo. Runo and Tigrerra had helped Dan and Drago save Earth and restore Vestroia.

Now Tigrerra was fighting again — against the invaders.

"Focus, Baron," she told the young brawler. "We have a battle to win."

"You're right!" Baron cried. He grabbed her in his palm and threw her out onto the field. "Bakugan Brawl!"

The ball burst open as Tigrerra entered the battle, transforming into her true form on the field. She stood on two legs, a fierce, fighting jungle cat with claws and teeth as sharp as razors.

"Now you must answer to Tigrerra!" she growled.

"So," Helios said. "You are the last of the six fighting Bakugan."

"I may be the last, but Drago and Wavern sacrificed too much for this world to let you take it without a fight," Tigrerra shot back. "Right, Baron?"

Baron nodded. He loaded a card into a device strapped to his left arm.

"Ability Activate!" he yelled.

Tigrerra jumped high in the air. Gleaming metal claws sprang from her front paws.

"Velocity Fang!" she cried out.

She slammed into Helios — but the attack didn't seem to do any damage. "That tickles," Helios said with a wicked grin.

Tigrerra bounced back, confused. "What, you're still standing?"

"As long as the Burst Core is active, all of your power is useless, Tigrerra," Spectra gloated.

Tigrerra let out a low growl. Burst Core was an Ability Card that, when played, allowed Helios to block his opponent's special abilities.

Helios picked up Tigrerra by the throat and dangled her over the field. "Say good-bye to the last of the Bakugan Six," he said darkly.

Nemus got to his feet. "Baron, do something!"

"Right!" Baron yelled. "Ability Activate!"

Nemus pointed his staff at Helios. A bolt of golden light shot out and hit Helios in the back.

"No one can hide from the light of my Shining Force!" Nemus yelled.

The dragonoid turned his head. He looked annoyed, but not hurt.

"Don't you get it?" Spectra said. "Helios and I are —"

"INVINCIBLE!" Helios shouted, tossing Tigrerra

aside. She slammed into the ground, landing at Nemus's feet.

Spectra's pale eyes gleamed. "Ability Activate."

"General Quasar!" Helios roared.

Boom! Boom! Boom! Explosions rocked the battlefield as Helios hurled fireball after fireball at his opponents.

"Nemus, move!" Tigrerra yelled. She jumped up, knocking Nemus aside.

"Tigrerra!" Nemus cried.

The flames engulfed Tigrerra. There was no escape.

"I'm sorry, Drago," she said sadly. "I've failed you."

Defeated, Tigrerra turned back into a Bakugan ball. The ball bounced across the field and landed in Spectra's hand.

Not only had Baron lost the battle — he'd lost Tigrerra to the invaders.

CHAPTER 3

DRAGO'S PLEA

T igrerra, too?" Drago asked.

In his new form as the core of New Vestroia, Drago was a big glowing ball of energy. He didn't have eyes or ears, but because he was part of Vestroia he could still see and hear everything that happened on the world. Over the last few weeks he had slowly watched his friends fall to the invaders, one by one. Trapped in his energy form, Drago couldn't do anything to help.

"Is this to be my fate?" Drago cried into the darkness. "I ask you, ancestors, am I doomed to watch my friends fall defending the world I sacrificed everything to protect? Answer me!"

As he spoke, six figures appeared in the space around Drago. The Legendary Warriors of Vestroia were spirits who watched over the planet. Sometimes, they took physical form as Bakugan. In their true form, they looked like masked warriors in armor.

"We hear you, Drago, and we have come," said Apollonir. His armor was red and orange, with bladelike orange wings on the back.

"We are with you, in the core," said Oberus. Small and green, with delicate antennae, she had a pleasant, musical voice.

"The Ancient Warriors of Vestroia?" Drago asked. "Then there is hope!"

A warrior in glowing white armor nodded. "There is always hope," said Lars Lion. "Each of us sacrificed much to save our world."

"Just as you have sacrificed, oh courageous Drago," said Exedra, a towering figure in black and purple. Red horns grew from the top of his head.

"But now New Vestroia faces a danger unlike any other," said Oberus.

"And in this time of need, we ask you to sacrifice once again, young Dragonoid," added Apollonir. "You are the only one who can save our world now."

"But what can I do?" Drago asked. "I'm not a dragonoid anymore. I am the Perfect Core that balances and binds the world. If I were to leave, New Vestroia would separate and that would mean the end of everything."

Frosch, a warrior in blue robes, spoke up next. He was smaller than most of the others, and had the appearance of an old man with a white beard. He carried a blue staff. "There is a way," he said. "If we combine our power you can separate from the Core and regenerate your body."

"But what of New Vestroia?" Drago asked.

"You must leave behind enough energy to sustain the Core, Drago," Exedra answered. "But it can be done."

"Then we must do it right away!" Drago said.

Lars Lion nodded. "Agreed. But you must accept the consequences."

"Once you are separated from the Core, you will not be as powerful as you once were, and you will not look the same," Frosch explained.

"None of that matters," Drago insisted. "I'd give anything to battle for our world again. Help me, ancient warriors. Help me to save New Vestroia!"

The sixth warrior spoke for the first time. Clayf sat on a stone throne. An earth-colored mask covered his face. He wore white robes, and his breastplate looked as though it had been chiseled from solid rock.

"Very well, Drago," Clayf said with a chuckle.

Each warrior extended an arm. A jolt of electrified energy shot out from each warrior, zapping the Perfect Core.

The light of each warrior was a different color, representing each of the powers of Vestroia. Lars Lion's was yellow Haos light; Oberon's green energy held the power of the wind; Frosch's Aquos energy was the bright blue of clear water; Clayf's orange energy represented Subterra and the power of earth; Fiery red Pyrus energy flew from Apollonir's fingers; and Exedra blasted Drago with purple Darkus power.

Drago screamed as the transformation took place. "I feel like I'm being ripped apart!"

The Perfect Core took the form of a red ball of light. Each of the warriors pointed upward, sending Drago shooting through a portal in space.

"You must endure, Drago!" Frosch called out.

Drago wasn't sure he *could* endure. He had never felt such pain, as if every part of his body were exploding, all at once.

The Perfect Core took the form of a red ball of light. Each of the warriors pointed upward, sending Drago shooting through a portal in space. He lost all sense of his surroundings. Then, suddenly, he could hear Apollonir's voice.

"It is done," Apollonir said. "Remember, Drago. You cannot find victory alone. You will need a partner."

"Ha! I don't have to choose," Drago called behind him. "There's only one human I would ever call partner!"

ack on Earth, Dan walked through a park with his friends Marucho, Julie, and his sort-of girl-friend, Runo. All three of them were excellent Bakugan brawlers who had helped Dan and Drago save the world before. Dan had called them as soon as he suspected something bad was going on in New Vestroia.

But one important member of the group wasn't there.

"I left a message for Shun, but he hasn't returned my call," Dan complained. "He never does. Is that a ninja thing, or what?"

"You probably lost your cool and annoyed him again," said Runo. She had blue-green eyes and bright blue hair that she wore in pigtails.

Dan spun around. "I never lose my cool!" he said angrily.

Julie and Marucho watched their friends argue.

"Boring!" said blonde-haired, blue-eyed Julie in a singsong voice. "Are those two pretending to hate each other again? Change the channel!"

Beside her, Marucho laughed. The youngest and shortest of the brawlers, Marucho wore big eyeglasses and a school uniform.

"Why don't you try Shun one more time?" Runo asked.

Dan flipped open his cell phone. "I've already called him, like, a billion times," he replied. He dialed one more time and then frowned. "I can't connect. Something's interfering."

As he spoke, dark clouds suddenly appeared in the blue sky. Thunder rumbled and a jagged bolt of lightning struck the path just in front of them. Runo and Dan screamed and dove to escape being hit.

When they got back on their feet, the clouds had vanished and a swirling portal of blue light glowed on the pathway in front of them. A small red ball shot out of the portal and landed on top of an overturned garbage can, bouncing once before it stopped moving.

"Whoa!" Dan cried. "It can't be!"

"Sure it can, Dan," came a voice from the ball with a hearty laugh. "Everything is possible!"

The ball opened up to reveal a Dragonoid Bakugan with a long neck and wings.

"A Bakugan?" Runo was excited and confused at the same time. All of the Bakugan had left Earth once Vestroia was restored.

"But which one?" Dan wondered.

The Bakugan jumped into Dan's open hands.

"Hello, Daniel!" he said.

Runo gasped in surprise.

"Drago? Is it you, man?" Dan asked.

"Of course!" Drago said happily, hopping up and down in Dan's palm. "Who else could make an entrance like that?"

Dan was so excited he jumped up and down. "Drago's back! Drago's back! Drago's back!"

Julie and Marucho ran up.

"Is it true?" Julie asked.

"I can't believe it. Is he *really* back?" Marucho asked.

"He is!" Dan said happily. "Take a look."

He held out Drago so everyone could see.

"It's good to see you, brawlers. All of you," Drago said.

"Hooray! Hooray!" Julie cheered. Then she leaned down to get closer to Drago. "Drago, can Gorem come visit, too?"

"And what about Tigrerra?" Runo asked.

"How's Preyas?" Marucho chimed in. "I can't wait to see him again, Drago!"

Drago's voice became serious. "I'm sorry. I'm not here for a visit," he explained. "I'm here to ask for your help."

"What's happened?" Dan asked.

"New Vestroia has been invaded," Drago told them. "Most of the Bakugan have been captured and enslaved."

The brawlers gasped in horror.

"Are you kidding?" Dan asked.

"It's no joke," Drago replied. "That's why I came to you, Dan. I can't save them alone."

He turned and looked at Dan. "Will you help me, Dan?"

"Hello! You bet I will!" Dan replied without hesitating. "We'll make those 'spaced' invaders wish they'd never heard of Dan and Drago!"

Runo pumped her fist in the air. "And Runo!"

"And Julie!" Julie cried.

"Yes!" Marucho agreed. "We're all here to help, Drago."

"Thank you," Drago said. "The first thing you can do to help me is to turn around. All of you."

"Okay," Julie said with a shrug. She, Runo, and Marucho turned their backs on Dan and Drago.

"Since when was he so shy?" Runo asked.

Drago hopped onto Dan's shoulder. "Dan, I can't take the others," he whispered. "It's got to be you and me alone."

Dan looked at Drago in surprise.

"I'm sorry," he said. "We have to go now. Hurry."

Drago nodded toward the portal, and Dan understood. "Okay," he said with a nod.

Then he quickly ran inside the spinning portal.

Runo and Julie had no idea what had happened.

"Can we turn around yet, Drago?" Julie asked.

"How long does it take for a Bakugan to change, anyway?" Runo asked.

Impatient, the two girls turned around. The portal was gone. All that remained was a small crater dug into the path in front of them.

"Heeey, those rats ditched us!" Runo cried, shaking her fist.

"Either that or they're digging a pool!" Julie joked — but she wasn't happy. "No fair! Come on, you guys, take us with you!"

"I never get to save the world — except for that one time!" Runo yelled.

Dan flew through the portal with Drago in hand.

"Sorry, Dan. I don't want to get you in trouble with the others," Drago said.

"We're cool, Drago," Dan told him.

"I'm taking a big risk contacting humans again," Drago explained. "I know I can count on you but I can't put the others in harm's way. It's just too dangerous."

"Sounds more like you're hogging all the fun!" came a familiar voice behind them.

Dan and Drago looked behind them — to see Marucho flying toward them!

"Marucho?" Dan asked in surprise.

"No sneaking away on me!" Marucho said. "I'm coming with you guys. Isn't it awesome?"

The portal dropped Dan, Marucho, and Drago into a vast, dry desert. Dusty ground stretched out as far as they could see. Tall rocks rose up from the sand instead of trees and plants.

"So this is New Vestroia?" Dan asked in disbelief.

"I remember it being kind of greener," Marucho said.

Dan looked down at Drago, who was perched on his shoulder. "Tell us what happened to your home, Drago."

"It was paradise . . . before they came," Drago said darkly.

"Sorry, Drago," Dan said. "You must have felt pretty helpless having to watch all of this happen."

Drago nodded. "I did," he said. "Let me start at the beginning. One day, with no warning, alien ships descended upon our land. The invaders called themselves the Vestals and they came to stay. They planted their cities, one after another, in our ground with no regard for life as we knew it."

Dan gazed at the sky, imagining what it must have looked like, filled with unfriendly ships.

"They transmitted a destructive energy field across New Vestroia," Drago continued. "An energy that changed the molecular balance of everything in its path. This energy also transformed all the Bakugan back into spheres."

"Is that so they could overpower you easily?" Dan asked.

Drago nodded. "Yes. Then they began to capture all the Bakugan. One after another. Preyas . . . Gorem . . . Skyress . . . Hydranoid . . . Tigrerra. All gone." He sadly lowered his head.

"But that's just plain rude!" Marucho protested.

"That's so rank!" Dan agreed. He angrily waved his arms around. "If they think they can just waltz onto this planet and take over the Bakugan, then they'll have to answer to me. You hear me?"

A strange voice answered him.

"I hear you, but what are you gonna do about it?"

Dan turned to see two guys standing on top of a big rock. One was kind of short, with a pointy chin, blue eyes, and wavy purple hair. He wore a fancy-looking jacket, puffy pants tucked into boots, and fingerless black gloves.

The other looked bigger and tougher, with spiky red hair, a chiseled face, and an angry expression. He wore a white vest with a high white collar over a sleeveless black top and black pants.

Dan's eyes narrowed when he saw them. Vestals!

"Just who I was looking for," he said.

The bigger one grunted. "Go home to your toys, children."

"You better go back where you came from," Dan warned.

The purple-haired guy laughed. "Surrender to you? This I gotta see."

"Pretty big talk for a little kid," said the big guy. "Come on, show me whatcha got."

Dan was fired up for battle. "I'll send you home crying to your mommies!" he yelled, pointing at the Vestals.

"Yeah, you better pay attention to what he says," Marucho added. "Dan and Drago are the greatest Bakugan brawlers in the universe."

The purple-haired guy looked up at his partner. "What do you think, Volt? Should we waste some time teaching these little squirts a lesson? It should be easy. They don't have gauntlets."

"What are gauntlets?" Dan asked, and then he shrugged. "Eh, who needs them? All I need is Drago."

The Vestal with purple hair burst out laughing. He fell on his back, kicking wildly. "Toooooo funny!"

Suddenly, the roar of an engine filled the air. A yellow motorcycle came flying over a boulder behind Dan and Marucho. The boys screamed and jumped forward to get out of the way.

The bike landed in the dirt, skidded to a halt, and then the rider turned the bike around. She had wavy red hair, blue eyes, and wore a short-sleeved white jacket over a brown shirt and pants.

"Not her again," muttered the purple-haired guy.

"I don't know where you come from or what you're doing here, but you'll need a gauntlet to battle in New Vestroia," the girl said.

"I don't take orders from the Vestals!" Dan said angrily.

"I lead the Bakugan Brawler Resistance," the girl told him. "My name is Mira."

CHAPTER 6

ABILITY ACTIVATE!

ira tossed a gauntlet at Dan. It was long and flat and tapered at both ends. She had one just like it strapped onto her left forearm.

Dan caught the gauntlet.

"You're pretty . . . and scary," Marucho remarked.

Mira ignored the comment. "First let's see if you can keep up . . . against the Vexos."

"The Vexos?" Dan asked.

"Yes, they're Vestal's top Bakugan brawlers," Mira explained. "The big one with no brains is Volt. The baby who thinks he's cool is Lync."

"Hey, watch your mouth!" Lync protested.

"Like he said," Volt added.

"They're mine!" Dan said confidently.

Mira stepped up to him. "So, human, tell me — are you a chicken or a brawler?"

"I'm no chicken!" Dan cried. "Come on, let me at those creeps. I'll show them!" He strapped the gauntlet to his arm.

Mira nodded and turned toward the Vexos. "Fine. Let's go."

Volt and Lync jumped off of the rock. "Finally, the talking stops!" Lync said. "We accept your challenge."

"It's almost too easy to be fun," Volt said.

"Want fun?" Mira asked with a gleam in her eye. She raised her arm and pressed a button on top of her gauntlet.

"Gauntlet activated," announced the device in a mechanical voice. A metal tray slid out. Mira placed an Ability Card in it, and the tray slid closed. The back of the card appeared on the face of the gauntlet. It glowed, a sign that the card was ready for play.

"Gauntlet Power Strike!" she yelled.

Volt and Lync each loaded a card into their gauntlet.

"Power Strike!" they both shouted.

Dan fumbled with his gauntlet. "How's this work?" he wondered out loud. He saw the red button on top. "Push this?"

The tray opened up, just like Mira's had. *"Gauntlet activated."*

"Now the Ability Card," Dan said. He placed the card in the tray. It slid closed and the card began to glow.

"Oh yeah! I rock!" Dan cheered.

Mira was not impressed. *This dweeb has no idea what he's doing,* she thought. *I can't believe I've sunk this low.*

"Show them what you're made of, Dan!" Marucho called out.

Dan pumped his fist in the air. "Right!"

"I'm first, okay kiddies?" Lync asked. "Gate card set!"

He tossed a card out onto the field. The card lit up the space between the brawlers with green light, setting the area of play.

Then Lync tossed a green Bakugan in his hand. "Bakugan Brawl!"

He tossed the ball onto the field. "Bakugan Stand!"

The ball transformed into a big green Bakugan that looked like a bug with wings and three large horns growing from each snout. Each of the horns was topped with a sharp, silver blade.

"Ventus Fly Beetle!" Lync announced proudly.

Fly Beetle's wings flapped and it hovered over the field.

"Bakugan Brawl!" Volt yelled, throwing out a Bakugan ball. "Bakugan Stand! Haos Verias!"

Volt's ball transformed into an ape with white fur carrying a glowing staff. Verias made monkeylike noises as it twirled the staff around like a skilled ninja preparing for battle.

Volt sneered at Mira and Dan. "What are you waiting for? Christmas?"

I don't need an invitation to crash your party, Mira thought. She turned to Dan. "I'll take the lead," she said in a low voice. "You follow. Watch carefully."

"Hey, kid! When are you gonna stop hiding behind Mira and come out and play?" Lync taunted.

"Why, you!" Dan said angrily.

"Calm down, hot head!" Mira warned.

But Dan was all fired up. "No one calls *me* a coward!"

"We do! Ha ha!" Verias said with a laugh.

Dan opened his palm and gazed down at Drago's Bakugan ball.

"Ready, pal?" Dan asked.

"Ready," Drago said with a nod.

"Bakugan Brawl!" Dan yelled, throwing Drago onto the field. "Bakugan Stand!"

The ball exploded into a wall of fire that blasted

Verias, instantly defeating him. Verias transformed back into a sphere.

"Fly Beetle! Look out!" Lync warned.

Lync's Bakugan tried to fly away, but Dan was too fast. He loaded an Ability Card into his gauntlet.

"Ability Card set," the gauntlet informed him.

"Ability Activate!" Dan yelled. "Burning Dragon!"

The wall of fire changed form in front of their eyes, and a dragon made of flame emerged and chased Fly Beetle across the sky.

Wham! Drago slammed into Fly Beetle, and the big bug came crashing down to the ground.

"I don't believe it!" Mira cried. "He beat them both!"

Drago swooped down and landed in front of Dan. The flames faded, and Dan saw Drago in his new Dragonoid form for the first time: long neck and tail, two sets of huge wings, one long horn on the end of his snout, and a diamond-shaped jewel on his chest. His scales were bright red, his belly was white, and the markings on his body were golden yellow.

"Drago! How does it feel to be back in the saddle?" Dan asked.

"Great, Dan!" Drago replied. "I've missed you, partner!"

CHAPTER 7

WILDA ROCKS!

Drago transformed back into a sphere and bounced back into Dan's hand. Dan felt great. Battling with Drago was the best feeling in the world.

Mira looked down at her gauntlet. *Lync's life gauge dropped by half with just one blow!* she realized. *Dan's the most powerful brawler I've ever seen!*

"Hey, what is a life gauge, anyway?" Dan asked.

"Whatever power level you lose in battle, your life gauge goes down as well," Mira explained. "And when it hits zero, you've lost."

Dan nodded thoughtfully. This gauntlet was a whole new way of playing.

"I like this," Marucho chimed in. "A Bakugan breakthrough: a clean, clear way to decide who the winner will be."

Across the battlefield, Volt was glaring at Lync.

"What are you looking at?" Lync asked.

"A partner who's a showoff," Volt said. "Come on, we've got to win this game."

"I *know* that Bakugan," Lync told him. "Drago . . . Drago. Where have I heard that name?"

"It's my turn to play!" Mira said. "Gate Card set!"

She threw out a Gate Card, setting up a new round of battle. Then she hurled a brown Bakugan ball onto the field.

"Bakugan Stand! Subterra Wilda!"

The Bakugan that emerged from the ball looked like a giant made of stone, with fists like boulders and two massive round rocks for shoulders. Two curved horns grew from either side of her head.

"Bakugan Brawl!" Volt cried, throwing out another white Bakugan ball. "Bakugan Stand! Haos Freezer!"

Volt's Bakugan looked like a six-legged octopus with a gleaming white body. Its large, cylinder-shaped head looked more mechanical than natural, with four purple eyes and a red upside-down triangle in the center of its forehead.

"I've got your number, Mira!" Lync promised. "Bakugan Brawl!"

Lync threw a green ball onto the field. "Bakugan Stand! Ventus Atmos!"

Atmos looked like a large, beautiful bird of prey with green feathers. It let out a loud screech as it soared over the field.

"Gate card open!" Mira called out. "Subterra Reactor!"

Tall stone pillars rose up on the field.

"Power level increase detected," the gauntlet reported.

Now Wilda had 850 Gs of power — and Freezer and Atmos only had 350 each. Wilda had enough power to take down *both* Bakugan!

"You think you're so clever!" Lync said with a grin. "Ability Activate. Typhoon Chase!"

Atmos flapped its wings, and a strong wind whipped across the field as the bird's Gs jumped to 450.

"Power level increase."

"Man, he really is a blowhard!" Dan joked.

Mira loaded another card into her gauntlet. "Double Ability Activate. Power Winder plus Gun Lock!"

"No way!" Dan cried.

The two abilities merged, stealing 200 Gs from Atmos and transferring them to Wilda. Now Wilda had an impressive 1050 Gs.

Marucho was really impressed with Mira's strategy. "Amazing! She activated two abilities at the same time!" he said.

"Awesome," Dan agreed. "I didn't know it was possible."

"I'll take care of this one, kid," Mira assured him. "You've got a few things to learn."

"Say what?" Dan asked angrily. He sat down and folded his arms across his chest. "Fine, I'll just sit here. There's so much I've got to learn from you, teacher," he said sarcastically.

Drago hovered in front of him. "Calm down."

"Yeah, calm down," Marucho repeated.

"Man, he is such a baby," Mira said. "That's his problem. Let's go! Wilda attack!"

Wilda charged across the field, knocking down stone pillars with her huge fists.

"Bring it!" Volt cried. "Ability Activate! Freeze Jail!"

Freezer raised a tentacle and aimed a blast of pulsating light at Wilda. The Subterra Bakugan froze on the spot.

Lync smiled. "You take too much for granted," he said smugly. "Abilities don't help if you can't use them. Go Atmos!"

"Freezer!" Volt commanded.

The two Bakugan charged toward Wilda, who was helpless to fight them off.

"Wilda!" Mira cried in alarm.

That's when Dan jumped into action. He hurled Drago into the battle. "Bakugan Stand!"

Drago landed in front of Wilda and exploded into a tornado of flames, pushing back Freezer and Atmos.

"Maybe you should watch and learn," Dan told Mira. "Time to activate ability . . . *double* ability, that is!"

Dan loaded two cards into his gauntlet. "Burst Shield plus Burning Dragon. Let's go, Drago!"

"Drago," Lync said with a gasp of surprise. Suddenly, he remembered where he had heard that name.

Drago flew into the air and transformed into a dragon made of fiery flames. Then he swooped down.

Bam! Bam!

He easily knocked Freezer and Atmos out of the battle.

Lync and Volt watched their life gauge drop.

"Power loss detected."

The two losing Bakugan turned back into spheres — and bounced into Dan's hand. Dan wasn't sure why he had ended up with the Vexos Bakugan, but it didn't matter right now. They were free!

"Oh yeah! That did the trick," Dan cheered.

"Nice work with the gauntlet, Dan," Marucho said.

Dan felt great. "I'm back in the battle!"

Mira was shocked. *Who is this human?* she thought. *He captured two Bakugan in one brawl and didn't even break a sweat. He used a gauntlet and executed a combination ability attack on his very first try. That should have taken hours of practice.*

"I remember now," Lync told Volt. "That, my friend, is one of the six fighting Bakugan who saved Vestroia. Meet Pyrus Dragonoid!"

Mira gasped. "Then you two must be . . ."

"I'm Dan Kuso, at your service," Dan said.

"I'm Choji Marakura, but call me Marucho," said Marucho.

"Dan . . . Marucho. Now it's clear. You're part of the six Bakugan brawlers," Mira said.

"Well, we're two of them, anyway," Dan said. "Whaddya think, Marucho? Sounds like we've become famous."

Marucho nodded. "Pretty cool, except we didn't even know it."

"Famous schmamous," Volt said with a snort. "They're still toast."

"Next time we'll get your autographs," Lync said with a laugh.

Then they quickly jumped over the boulder and ran off. Dan and Marucho climbed on top of the rock and watched them go.

"Sure, just run away!" Dan called out.

"Come back, cowards!" Marucho yelled.

Mira watched them both. *With these two on our side, just maybe we have a chance to save New Vestroia after all!*

ira walked over to her yellow motorcycle. "We should leave before they come back with reinforcements," she said. Dan and Marucho just stared at her.

"Well? Climb on," Mira said.

"As if!" Dan exclaimed. "With the way you drive?"

Mira shrugged. "Well if you're scared, you can just walk."

Dan and Marucho looked at each other. Barren desert surrounded them on all sides. They'd probably have to walk for miles.

They'd have to take their chances with Mira. They climbed on the bike and Mira sped across the sand.

Meanwhile, the news of Lync and Volt's defeat quickly got back to the rest of the Vexos. They flew over New Vestroia in a Vestor destroyer, a large black spaceship.

The six Vexos gave a report to the Vestal ruler, Prince Hydron. His face appeared on a large screen in the ship's control room. He was a young man, with feathery white hair, pale blue eyes, and a thin face.

"Intriguing," Prince Hydron said thoughtfully. "So you're sure you've found the last of the six Bakugan?"

"Yes," Spectra replied. As the leader of the Vexos fighters, he spoke for the group. "It seems that the beast has joined forces with the Bakugan Brawlers Resistance."

"That's good," Hydron said, twirling a lock of his own hair. "I'd hate to take him down without a fight. Crush the Resistance and bring the Dragonoid to me."

He pressed a button on the arm of his throne and a wall rose up behind him to reveal a large room. The five Bakugan who had fought with Drago were frozen like statues, and arranged around the room like decorations. Skyress, Hydranoid, Preyas, Gorem, and Tigrerra — all had been captured, except for Drago.

Prince Hydron grinned. "I want to complete my collection."

Back on Earth, Runo and Julie were frustrated they hadn't been able to go to New Vestroia with Dan and

Marucho. But there was nothing they could do. They had to get back to their normal lives.

That meant working at Runo's family restaurant. Julie put on a yellow apron and some roller skates and waited on tables, zipping back and forth down the aisles.

"Have no fear, Julie's here to take your order!" she said, skidding to a stop at a table with four teen-age boys.

"How about an orange soda?" asked one boy.

"No, take my order first, Julie!" said another.

Julie giggled. "Don't fight, guys. I'll get to all of you!"

The boys blushed and sighed. Runo found herself getting angry. Every time Julie helped out at the restaurant every male customer acted like an idiot.

"Stop playing around and take some orders!" Runo snapped.

Julie looked over her shoulder. "Unlike some people, I know how to have fun and work at the same time."

That was it. Runo's face turned beet red. The customers knew what was coming. They had seen her lose her temper before — and it wasn't pretty.

"Run!" yelled one of the boys.

Everyone stampeded out of the restaurant.

"I know how to have fun!" Runo screamed.

"Oh, yeah," Julie shot back. "You're a laugh riot!"

"I'll fight anyone who says I'm not fun!" Runo shrieked.

Julie quickly skated into the kitchen.

Gradually, the customers came back, Runo calmed down, and Julie came out of hiding. The rest of the day went quietly, and soon it was time to close up.

Julie pulled a postcard from her apron. "Look, Runo! I got a postcard from Billy."

Julie's childhood friend, Billy, had been a top Bakugan brawler.

"Really? How's he doing?" Runo asked.

"He's traveling the world to learn from the greatest athletes he can find," Julie explained. "He's in Spain right now. I bet he's an awesome bullfighter."

Then Julie noticed Runo's sad face. "You haven't heard from Dan lately, have you?" she asked.

"Who cares about Dan?" Runo said angrily. Then she softened and reached under the register, taking out a photo of Dan. "If he wants to ditch us and run off with Drago, well that's fine by me."

But really, it wasn't fine. Runo missed him.

"Just be careful, Dan," she said with a sigh.

CHAPTER 9

MIRA'S STORY

Dan and Marucho held on tightly as Mira raced across the desert. Dan knew Mira was on the side of the Bakugan, but he didn't really understand what she was up to.

"Hey, Mira, aren't you a Vestal just like those Lync and Volt dudes?" he asked.

"I may be a Vestal but I'm not like them," Mira replied.

"So that's why you lead the Bakugan Brawlers Resistance?" Marucho asked.

"Sort of," Mira said. "It's a long story but I guess it's important for you to know exactly what happened.

"You might not believe it, but one day Bakugan cards fell from the sky, as if by magic. And from them came the Bakugan themselves," Mira began.

"The same thing happened to us!" Dan exclaimed.

"Yes," Mira agreed. "When Dr. Michael's dimension transporter malfunctioned it created a rift in our world, too."

"Looks like you were connected to Vestroia just like we were," Marucho remarked.

Mira nodded. "Our world was too crowded. So when our king discovered New Vestroia, he conquered the planet and colonized it with our overflowing population. Once the invasion was over, we built Bakugan battle arenas in their cities. We were eager to play with our powerful new 'pets.'

"Everyone went crazy for the thrilling Bakugan Battles," Mira went on. "Tickets sold like wildfire. You couldn't get one now if you tried."

"Hmph," Drago snorted from his perch on Dan's shoulder. "You treat us like animals. The Bakugan were living in peace when you Vestals attacked. Now they're enslaved and forced to battle for the amusement of the Vestal people. How can you be so cruel?"

"We didn't know," Mira explained. "The people have never been told that the Bakugan are intelligent creatures."

"So you people think the Bakugan are like pets who do tricks for them?" Dan asked.

"Yes," Mira said. "And so did I . . . until the day I discovered the truth."

Mira would never forget that day. She'd never suspected when she woke up that morning that her whole world was about to change.

Mira rode her motorcycle up to the underground entrance of her father's lab. She thought she'd pay a visit and say hi, maybe even see what new projects he was working on. She skidded to a halt in front of two startled security guards wearing green uniforms. They quickly blocked her path.

Mira lowered her sunglasses and grinned. "You guys wouldn't want to keep me out, would you?"

The guards recognized her.

"You're Professor Clay's daughter!" one guard said. "Sorry, ma'am."

"Hang on," said the other guard, "I'll get Professor Clay on the line."

"Please don't," Mira said. The guards looked at her quizzically, and she gave them a wink. "I want to surprise him. That's okay, right?"

The guards smiled. "Oh sure."

"Fine by us!"

Mira parked inside and made her way up to her father's lab, where she was greeted by an assistant in a lab coat and goggles. She followed him down the hallway, and suddenly, the whole building began to shake. Mira gripped the wall for support.

Whoa? What was that? Mira wondered.

A blinding white light bathed the hallway. Up ahead, Mira saw a window looking down into her father's lab. It looked like a lightning storm was brewing inside!

Curious, Mira ran to the window.

"Mira, wait!" the assistant cried out.

Mira looked down and saw Hydranoid, a dragonlike Bakugan with three heads, caught in the middle of the lightning. The Hydranoid roared in pain.

Mira was horrified. "Father, what are you doing here?" she whispered.

The assistant grabbed her by the arm. "I'm going to have to ask you to leave, Miss Mira."

But Mira broke away and ran to find her father.

"Hey! Hey!" the assistant called after her.

Professor Clay stood in front of a control panel, flanked by two more assistants.

"Can't you keep him quiet?" Clay asked crossly.

Another jolt of electricity zapped Hydranoid, and the Bakugan cried out again.

"Do your worst, destroyer!" Hydranoid yelled. "We will never give up!"

Mira stopped. "That Bakugan, it spoke!"

Mira confronted Professor Clay that night in their apartment. He stared down at the table, unable to meet his daughter's eyes.

"It's not right, Father," Mira told him. "You said we were colonizing an uninhabited world, but that's not true. We're the invaders, aren't we?"

Professor Clay was silent.

"Well, aren't you going to say anything?" Mira asked.

"This is not your concern, Mira," he said with annoyance. Then he stood up and walked away.

"Father!" Mira cried, but Professor Clay did not look back.

"My father didn't even care," Mira told Dan, Drago, and Marucho. "But I did. I was alone. But someone needed to help the Bakugan. So I got together with people who felt the same way I did. We started the Bakugan Brawlers Resistance and we've been fighting to free your Bakugan ever since.

"But the Vexos champions are strong," Mira went on.

"Volt Luster is their top Haos Brawler. Gus Grav is a weasel, but a powerful Subterra brawler. Mylene Farrow is the leading Aquos brawler. She's devious. You've met Lync Volan, the top Ventus brawler. He'll do anything to win. Shadow Prove is the top Darkus brawler. He's brutal and cruel. And the most deadly of all, Spectra Phantom, number one Pyrus brawler.

"The six Vexos are champions of all six Bakugan attributes," Mira said. "They're stronger than us."

"It must be hard to fight your own people," Dan said.

Drago nodded. "I'm glad to hear there is honor among some of the Vestals."

Marucho smiled. "Yeah!"

Mira smiled back. "That means a lot, coming from you guys. Hey, we're almost there."

"Where?" Dan asked. All he could see were mountains on either side of them.

"Straight ahead!" Mira told him.

Dan craned to look around Mira's head and saw a hideout tucked into a corner of the mountainside, a white building with what looked like blocks stacked on top of each other.

"Whoa! So cool!"

s they pulled up to the hideout, a guy with spiky hair ran out and Mira had to slam on the brakes to avoid hitting him. It was Baron, the young Resistance fighter who had lost Tigrerra to Spectra.

"Welcome back!" Baron called out, waving.

"Hello, Baron," Mira said. "Let me introduce you to our guests." She nodded back to Dan and Marucho.

Baron's blue eyes widened. "The Masters!"

"Masters?" Dan was confused.

"I think he fell on his head," Marucho quipped.

But Baron was just fine. "I know exactly who you are. Dan Kuso and Marucho Marakura, Bakugan Brawling Masters!"

Mira was so embarrassed she covered her face with her hands. Baron bowed to Dan and Marucho.

"I'm Baron, at your service!"

"Uh, hi, Baron," Dan said.

"Pleased to meet you, I think," Marucho said with a laugh.

Baron straightened up. "The pleasure is all mine!" He reached out with both hands and started shaking Dan's and Marucho's hands. He shook them so hard that the two boys toppled off of the bike!

Dan slowly sat up, groaning and brushing dirt off of his red jacket. Drago flew out of Dan's pocket and hovered over the bike.

"I've never seen anyone so happy," Drago remarked.

Baron ran to the bike to get closer to Drago — and stepped on Dan and Marucho! But he didn't even notice. He stared at Drago in amazement.

"And you must be Master Drago!"

"That's me," Drago said pleasantly.

Now it was Baron's turn to hide his face in his hands. "I can't believe I embarrassed myself in front of the greatest Bakugan in the universe!"

Mira stepped off of her bike. "You have to excuse Baron. He's one of your biggest fans. He knows all about how you saved Vestroia and created New Vestroia. He even has a poster of you up on his bedroom wall."

Baron helped Dan and Marucho to their feet. "Sorry about that. I guess I got carried away."

"It's cool, man," Dan said. "We get recognized all the time. It's just part of the job. Stick around and I'll show you some of my battle strategy."

"I think I might faint!" Baron swooned.

Marucho whispered to Drago. "Great. Like Dan's ego wasn't big enough before!"

"Some things never change," Drago agreed, and Marucho giggled.

"So where is Ace?" Mira asked Baron.

"He said he had something to take care of," Baron replied.

"Up here!"

A guy about Mira's age stood on top of a large rock. He had shaggy, pale-blue hair, violet eyes, and wore a purple jacket with long sleeves over white pants.

"Ace!" Mira said in surprise.

"Sooo sorry," Ace said in a voice that didn't sound sorry at all. "I didn't mean to interrupt your bragging."

Dan glared at him. "What's your problem?"

"Get it together, Ace," Mira warned. "We've got company."

"Yeah, smarten up," Baron added. "Do you have any idea who these people are?"

"And they can go back to where they came from," Ace said. "We don't need their help. We'll free the Bakugan alone."

Mira was dismayed. "Ace."

"You disappoint me, Mira," Ace said. "I thought you were a true Vestal warrior, that you were gonna make a difference. Now you invite a couple of Earth dweebs to join the Resistance? You're just a starstruck fan girl!"

"Watch it!" Dan stepped forward, seething with anger. "We won't walk away if the Bakugan need us."

"Well said," Drago agreed.

"Too bad," Ace said. "We don't need any of your help to rescue all of the captured Bakugan. This is none of your business, so take your friend and go home!"

Dan gritted his teeth. He wasn't going anywhere. Why was this guy being so thick-headed?

"No, Ace," Mira said firmly. "To free the Bakugan we need all the help we can get. We don't have time for one of your ego trips."

A small smile crossed Ace's face. "Just humor me," he said. "The human should have to prove himself."

Ace slowly raised his arm. His fist was closed. He opened it to reveal a black and purple Bakugan ball. He held the ball between his fingers.

"What do you say, *Master*?" he asked Dan.

"Come on," Dan replied in disbelief. They were supposed to be working together — not fighting each other.

"Beat Percival and you can join the Bakugan Brawlers Resistance," Ace promised.

"Whoa," Baron said.

Dan turned to his Bakugan. "Drago?"

"I'm up for it!" Drago replied. He jumped off the bike and landed in Dan's hand.

"Okay, Ace," Dan said with a grin. "We'll take you on!"

CHAPTER 11

THE POWER OF PERCIVAL

Dan and Ace faced each other across the desert. A strong wind whipped up around them. Marucho, Mira, and Baron stood on the sidelines to watch.

"Why are those two battling each other?" Baron wondered. "They're on the same side."

"I guess they just have to get it out of their system," Mira said.

"Yeah, before they destroy each other," Marucho said worriedly.

Ace pointed at Dan. "Now remember this, when the Bakugan Brawlers Resistance battles the Vexos, we're not just playing childish games. We're fighting to free the Bakugan. In order to get the stolen Bakugan back, our power has to be at least five hundred points higher than our opponents."

"So that's why the Vexos Bakugan returned to me when I won," Dan realized.

"So if I win, I take your Drago. Agreed?" Ace asked.

"That's fine by me as long as I get your Percival when I beat you," Dan said confidently. "Are you scared?"

Ace just laughed. "Dream on. There's no way that's gonna happen."

Dan growled through gritted teeth. Both boys loaded their gauntlets.

"Gauntlet Power Strike!" Dan and Ace cried out at the same time.

Ace tossed a card onto the field. "Gate Card Set!"

"Now let's see what you've got, oh great master," Ace said sarcastically. "Just don't say I didn't warn you. You ready?"

"Always!" Dan shot back.

Ace held up Percival's Bakugan ball, and Dan held up Drago. They both tossed out their Bakugan.

"Bakugan Brawl!" they yelled together. "Bakugan Stand!"

A tornado of swirling purple and black light emerged from Percival's sphere. Drago's sphere burst into a tornado of fiery red flames. The two energy storms collided on the field, kicking up sand into the faces of the spectators.

Drago emerged from the storm and flew backward, slamming into a rock and landing at Dan's feet.

"Drago!" Dan yelled in alarm.

"Lucky shot," Drago grunted before he transformed back into a Bakugan ball.

Percival appeared through the dark, swirling winds. This humanoid Bakugan had armor on his purple body, a face like a dragon, and two horns growing on top of his head. A long, red cape flapped behind him. He hovered above the field, growling.

"This isn't going to be much of a contest. Look how high my power level is already," Percival boasted. Then he transformed back into a sphere and bounced back to Ace.

Dan checked his gauntlet to see that Percival had 450 Gs, higher than Drago's 400 — but not much higher. He could still turn this around.

"It's my turn," Dan said. "Gate Card Set!"

He added a Gate Card to the field. Then he and Ace threw out their Bakugan again.

"Bakugan Brawl!"

Mira was shocked. "What do they think they're doing?"

"If they shoot at the same time, then Drago will lose because his power level is lower!" Marucho said.

The spheres flew across the field and crossed paths in the middle. Drago's ball curved around Percival, missing him. Drago boomeranged back to Dan.

"Bakugan Stand! Drago!" Dan yelled.

"Bakugan Stand! Percival!" Ace cried.

The two Bakugan transformed.

Baron was impressed. "Whoa, did you catch that curve?"

"Dan must have put some spin on the ball when he shot it," Mira guessed. That move had kept Drago safe — for now.

"Pretty proud of yourself, huh?" Ace asked.

Dan grinned. "Ha!"

"Laugh it up," Ace said coolly. "I'm just getting started!"

He placed a card in his gauntlet.

"Ability Card Set."

"Ability Activate! Darkus Driver!" Ace announced.

Percival shot up into the sky like a rocket, flying into the clouds. Then he suddenly turned and zoomed back toward the ground, his body spinning like the bit of a drill.

"Not so fast!" Dan cried, loading a card into his gauntlet. "Ability Activate! Burning Dragon!"

Flames engulfed Drago's body. He flew up and collided with Percival in midair. Mira, Marucho, and Baron cried out in alarm as the fiery explosion rocked the desert.

When the smoke cleared, Drago was falling out of the sky. Dan checked his gauntlet. Drago's power had jumped by 200 Gs — but so had Percival's! Now Percival had 650 Gs, and Drago had 600.

"Snap!" Dan cried. "His power's still higher than mine!"

CHAPTER 12

A TRUCE

Dan, a little help, please?" Drago asked.

"Okay!" Dan replied. "Gate Card open! Pyrus Reactor!"

A wall of flames sprung up on the battlefield. Marucho jumped back to avoid the heat. The fire rose up and surrounded Drago.

"Power level increase," said the gauntlet, as Drago's power jumped to 700 Gs. Drago stopped spiraling out of control and zoomed across the field to attack Percival.

"Not finished yet!" Drago promised.

"Clever, but not clever enough!" Percival shot back. "Let's go!"

Ace loaded his gauntlet. "Ability Activate! Tri-Gunner!"

Percival hovered in the air in front of Drago, and Dan

saw he had a shield shaped like a dragon's head on each of his wrists. Percival crossed his arms, and the two mouths opened, shooting out purple light. Percival opened his own mouth and a third stream of light snaked out.

The three streams of light merged, becoming a pulsating ball of purple energy.

"Power level increase," the gauntlet reported. Dan looked at his gauntlet and saw that Percival's power jumped by 300 Gs. Percival had 950 Gs of power!

"Get ready, Drago!" Dan yelled. "Ability Activate! Burning Dragon!"

Drago's body burst into flames as his power level jumped by 200 to reach 950 Gs.

Marucho was nervous. "That's the third and final attack," he said. It was Dan's last chance to win the round.

"Their powers are even," Ace remarked.

Dan chuckled. "Think again. Fusion Ability Activate, Pyrus Slayer!"

A tunnel of flame whirled around Drago's body. He roared as the new power flowed through him.

"Drago power level increase," the gauntlet reported. Not only that, the move caused Percival to lose 100 Gs. Now it was Percival at 850, with Drago at 1250.

"No way!" Ace cried. "He used a combination Fusion Ability? I'll crush that!"

He loaded a card into his gauntlet. "Ability Activate! Night Explorer!"

Percival whirled around, sucking power from Drago. *"Power level decrease."*

But Drago's power only dropped down to 950 — still 100 Gs more than Percival.

Ace looked surprised. "No! It's not enough!"

Dan chuckled. It felt good to show Ace what he could do.

Drago zoomed toward Percival like a missile headed for its target.

Bam! He slammed into the Darkus Bakugan, and Percival exploded in a ball of purple light. His Bakugan ball landed at Ace's feet.

"Now we're even," Drago said.

Mira, Marucho, and Baron had dodged behind a rock to escape from the explosion. They cautiously stepped out when the dust cleared.

"How long can they keep this up?" Mira wondered.

"They're evenly matched so it's anyone's guess," said Marucho.

"Watch out," Baron warned. "Neither one is going to give in so they could end up obliterating each other."

He was right. Both Ace and Dan were more determined to win than ever. Ace threw the next Gate Card onto the field. He held Percival in his hand.

"Let's finish this, Percival," he said.

Percival nodded. "Once and for all!"

Ace glared across the field at Dan. "I'll show you power!" Then he tossed out his Bakugan.

Dan looked at Drago. "Are you ready to kick some Bakugan, Drago?"

"You can count on me, Dan!" Drago replied.

"Okay, let's do it. Bakugan Brawl!"

Dan threw Drago onto the field. He burst from his sphere, flapping his large wings.

Percival charged across the field and wrapped his long cape around Drago's body. Then he flew in circles, trapping Drago inside a glowing purple prison.

"Now!" Dan yelled.

Drago let out a battle roar and broke free, his body glowing with yellow light.

"Percival!" Ace cried.

The battle raged on . . . and on . . . and on. Dan and Ace expertly traded moves. Drago and Percival exchanged blows of fire and energy in midair. Power levels raised and fell — but the Bakugan were evenly matched.

Now the sun was setting. The barrage of attacks created a huge pit in the center of the field. Dan and Ace were exhausted and covered in dust.

"How long can they keep this up?" Baron asked.

"Unbelievable!" Marucho said. "Those two have been battling for over three hours."

Mira shook her head. "This has gone too far."

Ace taunted Dan across the field. "Come on. Bet you've had enough, haven't you? Just give up!"

"I'm just getting started!" Dan yelled back, his voice hoarse.

He held Drago in his hand. "Ready for another rumble?"

"Let's do it," Drago said.

Ace looked at Percival's Bakugan ball. "Let's finish them off."

"You bet," Percival replied.

Each brawler held up his Bakugan, ready to make the throw.

"Bakugan Braaaawl!" the boys yelled, but their voices were weak. They both ran forward . . . and fell facedown into the pit!

The boys were still at first. Then Ace began to laugh. Dan joined in.

Ace flipped over. "Man, you're off the rim!" he told Dan.

"Ha!" Dan replied. "And you're not?"

Drago popped out of his Bakugan ball. "You fought well, Percival."

"We'll settle this another time, Drago," Percival promised.

Mira, Marucho, and Baron ran to the edge of the pit. They looked down and saw the two brawlers laughing. Mira grinned.

"Looks like we have two new members."

CHAPTER 13

A PLAN IS FORMED

That night, the five brawlers gathered in the Resistance command center. Dan and Ace had cleaned themselves up, and Dan happily munched on a sandwich while Mira and the others explained more of what had been happening on the planet.

"Dimension Controller? What's that?" Dan asked.

"There are three dimensions," Mira explained. "Alpha, Beta, and Gamma. Their power changed the Bakugan back into balls."

"If we were to destroy those controllers, would that change the Bakugan back to their former selves?" Marucho asked.

"It's worth trying," Ace answered. "Battling Vexos will only get us so far. We need to hit them where it really, really hurts. That's why we've gotta wipe out all three controllers."

Baron pointed to a digital map of New Vestroia on the wall. The location of each of the controllers pulsated on the screen.

"But each of the Dimension Controllers is in the center of a city," Baron pointed out.

Mira studied the map. "So that means we have to hit the enemy in its lair. What do you think, Dan?"

Dan was too busy munching on his sandwich to reply.

"I couldn't agree with you more," Mira teased.

Dan finally swallowed his sandwich. "Sounds like my kind of mission!"

"Now that's the stuff," Mira said with a nod.

"I'm in!" Baron added.

Ace shook his head. "Gotta love a guy who doesn't overthink things."

Baron jumped into a white chair. "Brace yourself, everyone. We're taking off!"

Baron pressed a button on a screen in front of him, and the whole hideout began to shake.

"What's going on around here? An earthquake?" Dan asked.

But it was no earthquake — the hideout was transforming into a huge wheeled vehicle, capable of crossing over the toughest terrain.

"Next stop, Alpha City!" Baron announced.

Dan and Marucho ran to the windows, where they saw the mountains rolling past them.

"No way! This building is on the move?" Dan asked. "Must make it hard for the mailman to find your address."

"Relax," Mira said with a laugh. "This base turns into a tank."

"This is off the chain!" Dan said.

Ace took a seat at a control panel. "I think you'll like our technology. Even someone as slow as Dan can operate it!"

Dan wasn't insulted. He raised his arms in the air. "All right! This just keeps getting better and better! Right, Marucho?" Giddy, Dan picked up Marucho and lifted him over his head.

"Whoaaa! Let me down!" Marucho yelled. "I mean it, Dan! I might drool on you!"

Baron laughed. But watching the two boys made Mira thoughtful.

Dan and Marucho are always there for each other. Like brothers, she thought.

They reminded her of something — something painful to think about.

But she couldn't think about that now.

They had a world to save!